T0151114

N is for New York

written by kids for kids

WestWinds Press®

A

is for **Apple**

Green or red, sour or sweet,

Do you want one for a treat?

B is for **Baseball**

From Yankee Stadium to Frontier Field,
the game is quite fun. Come watch players
pitch and swing, maybe hit a home run!

C is for

Courage

Our brave public servants do their jobs with great courage. They work day and night and are seldom discouraged.

D is for **Dairy Farm**

Thank you cows for the milk and cheese.
These healthy foods are sure to please.

E

is for

the Empire State Building

This beautiful building,
so tall and bright,
I love to see it light
up the night.

F is for

Fall Colors

From Buffalo to Binghamton—
orange, red, yellow, brown—
You see so many colorful leaves
from town to town.

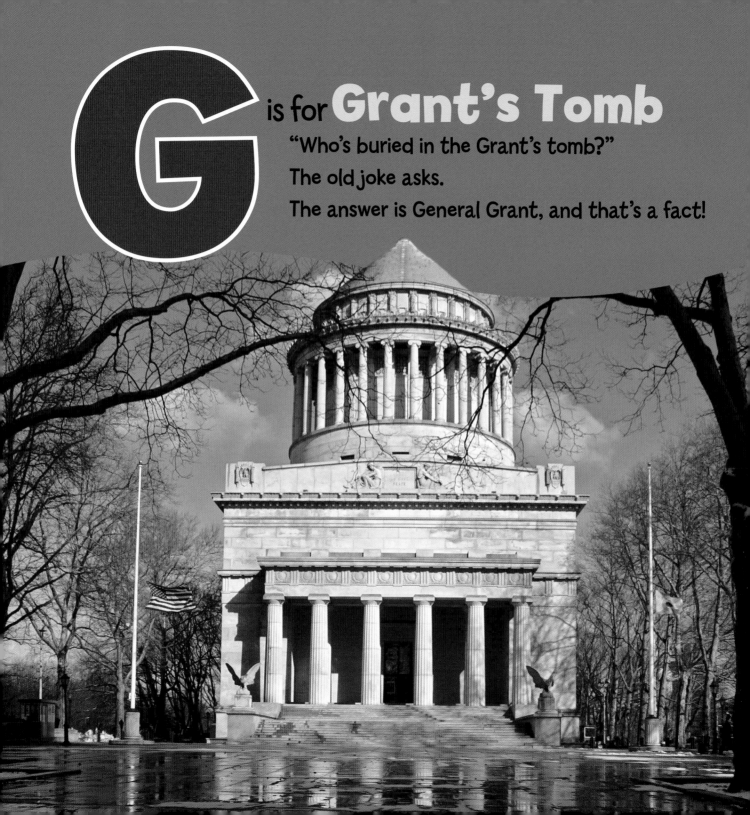

G is for Grant's Tomb

"Who's buried in the Grant's tomb?"
The old joke asks.
The answer is General Grant, and that's a fact!

H

is for **the Hamptons**

Beaches, boats and lots of water, It's a great place
to cool off when the weather gets hotter.

is for **Immigrants**
They come to America by air and by sea,
A new home for immigrants, the land of the free.

J is for the Jewish Heritage Museum

This museum is the place to see
How Jewish life is and used to be.

K is for Kayak

Water rages around my oar,
When I'm in my kayak,
far from shore.

L

is for

Ladybug

Our state bug is little,
it is red with black dots.
They do munch on plants,
but bite you? They will not!

M is for Manhattan

In the city skyscrapers
crowd your view.
Plays, music and art—
there is so much to do.

N is for Niagara Falls

People float past the falls
as they ride on the boat.
The water makes a huge splash
so remember your coat!

O

is for

Orient Point Lighthouse

It sits on the water and shines bright at night,
It helps find the shore so that they'll be alright.

P

is for

Peregrine Falcon

The peregrine falcon flies
so fast and so high from
its nest on tall skyscrapers,
it lets out its cry.

Q

is for **Queens**

Come see Staten Island,
Manhattan and Queens,
The Bronx and Brooklyn—
each has their own scene.

R

is for **River Otter**

I laugh when I watch the river otter
Titter, totter into the water.

S is for

Statue of Liberty

She stands for our liberty
and for our freedom,
Her lantern shines out
for all who may need them.

T is for Trout

Our state fish flashes silver and green.
Jumping and splashing and making a scene.

U is for

United Nations

Nearly two hundred nations
pledge to work together,
Keeping world peace,
now and forever.

V is for

Verrazano-Narrows Bridge

If you drive across the bridge from Staten Island
You'll get to Brooklyn so fast you'll be smilin'.

W

is for

White-tailed Deer

These deer are so gentle
with tails that are white
They wave their tails as
they jump out of sight.

is for X-mas

During Christmas, Rockefeller Center is the place to be. You can go ice-skating under the beautiful tree.

 is for

Yellow Taxi

The drivers will take you
anywhere you want to go,
But you'll have to pay,
so make sure you bring dough.

Z is for Bronx Zoo

Listen to tigers growl and monkeys call "Ooh! Ooh!" Come see all the animals at the Bronx Zoo.

Who Knew?

Apple
New York is the second largest apple-growing state in the country. They grow twenty-one different kinds, including seven created in New York (the Jonagold and Empire among them). On average New York produces twenty-five million bushels of apples a year. That's a lot of apple pie!

Baseball
New York has two Major League baseball teams. The Yankees began in 1903 as the Highlanders and didn't adopt the name we all know until 1913. In 1961, The New York Metropolitan Baseball Club Inc. formed. What a mouthful! They soon cut it down to a shorter nickname: "The Mets."

Courage
Nearly 26,000 volunteers helped in the rescue effort on September 11, 2001. Three-quarters came from the Police and Fire Departments of New York City. While many lost their lives that day, the amazing work of the volunteers helped save over 6,000 people. The National September 11 Memorial stands on the site where the World Trade Center Towers once stood.

Dairy
Moooove over Wisconsin, New York has more than 678,000 dairy cows! The state's 7,200 dairy farms produce 11.9 billion pounds of milk each year! Now where are you going to get enough cookies for all that milk?

Empire State Building
The Empire State Building is the third tallest building in America after the Willis Tower, and the Trump International Hotel and Tower. It is 1,250 feet tall! No surprise it's a natural lightning rod for the city. It gets zapped by lightning over 100 times a year. Shocking!

Fall Color
In the fall, leaves all over New York change color: red, yellow, and orange. The change happens because, as the days get shorter with the coming winter, there is less sunlight. Leaves use sunlight to make their food, chlorophyll, which is green. When they don't get enough sunlight, the green fades away, leaving bright fall colors.

Grant's Tomb
Who's buried in Grant's Tomb? General Ulysses S. Grant, of course! The leader of the victorious Union army in the Civil War was also two-time President of the United States. Built in 1897, Grant's tomb is the largest in America, even though it was built for just two people. (His wife is in there, too).

Hamptons
The Hamptons were first purchased from the Mantaukett Indians in exchange for one large black dog, some gunpowder and bullets, and a few blankets. Hopefully they were really beautiful blankets. In the 1800s the whaling industry took over the area, inspiring Herman Melville to write the most well known book about whales - Moby Dick.

Immigrants
Ellis Island was the gateway to America for many immigrants, but the very first was Annie Moore, a fifteen-year-old girl from Ireland on January 1, 1892. In its sixty-two years of operation, over twelve million people came into the U.S. through its historic doors. These immigrants helped make up the amazing diversity we call the "Great American Melting Pot."

Facts about the

Museum of Jewish Heritage

New York is home to the largest Jewish population outside of Israel. While some of the Museum of Jewish Heritage is dedicated to the Holocaust and the millions lost in World War II, it also celebrates the culture of the Jewish people that has continued to thrive since that dark time in history.

Kayaks

Kayaks were originally created by indigenous people living in the Arctic. Since then, kayaking has become a popular activity for people around the world. One great way to see New York is to jump in a kayak and paddle down the state's longest river – the Hudson. But, maybe not all in one day—it is 300 miles long.

Ladybugs

New York's state insect, the ladybug, is also called "lucky bug" in many cultures. People believe that if you catch one, make a wish, then blow it away, your wish will be granted. These beetles are especially lucky for gardeners. One little ladybug can eat up to sixty plant-munching aphids a day!

Manhattan

Manhattan is the most famous borough of New York City and home to many of the city's greatest attractions. It's only 333.8 square miles, but in that small space you'll find the Empire State Building, Broadway, the Statue of Liberty, Rockefeller Center, Grand Central Terminal, Central Park, and countless other amazing things to see and do. No wonder they get forty-seven million tourists each year!

Orient Point Lighthouse

Way out on the tip of Long Island, Orient Point Lighthouse has stood guiding ships around Oyster Point Reef and through the currents of Plum Gut since 1899. It's brown and white color led mariners to nickname it the "Coffee Pot." Maybe that helps the lighthouse keeper stay awake at night!

Peregrine Falcon

Although bluebirds are the state bird, peregrine falcons hold a special place in the hearts of New Yorkers. The falcons disappeared completely from the state in the 1960s. But with a lot of care and attention, including planning bridge construction around breeding season so that workers don't disturb nests, the falcons are coming back. In 1983 the first pair was discovered nesting on a bridge in Manhattan. Now there are more than sixty breeding pairs in the state and NYC has the largest urban population in the world!

Queens

New York City is divided into five boroughs—Queens, the Bronx, Brooklyn, Manhattan, and Staten Island—and each one has its own unique personality. Queens is the largest in size, but if each borough was its own city, every one of them would be in the top ten most populous cities in America.

Niagara Falls

Niagara Falls dumps over six million cubic feet of water every minute into the pools below. If you visit, be sure to wear a raincoat—that much water makes quite a splash! But not just water has gone over those falls—fifteen people and a cat have made the dangerous journey! One seven-year-old boy miraculously survived after he was swept over the falls in nothing but a life jacket!

great state of New York

River Otter

These cute critters are native to New York state. They find homes in New York's many bodies of water—eating fish, sliding in the mud, playing in the water, even burrowing through snow. They are great swimmers and can hold their breath for eight minutes! How long can you hold your breath?

Statue of Liberty

This symbol of America was actually made in France by sculptor Frederic Auguste Bartholdi. And the engineer of Paris's Eiffel Tower helped design her. Good thing, too: Lady Liberty is made of copper and steel and weighs 450,000 pounds. She towers more than 305 feet from pedestal to torch. Even her index finger is eight feet long!

Trout

The official freshwater fish of New York is the Brook Trout. It got its title in 1975 and can be found in lakes and ponds all over the Adirondack Mountains and in other streams throughout the state. The biggest trout caught in New York was 41-1/2 pounds. That would make quite a meal!

United Nations

The UN is an organization of 192 countries that work together on international issues. To help representatives from the different countries communicate, the UN has six official languages: Arabic, Chinese, English, French, Russian, and Spanish. To keep with the international theme, the land that the United Nations stands on is not part of Manhattan, New York, or even the United States. It is on international territory!

Verrazano-Narrows Bridge

Connecting Brooklyn and Staten Island is quite an achievement for one bridge. When it was built in 1964 it was the world's longest suspension bridge. It still ranks as one of the top ten longest at 4,260 feet. The bridge is so long, the two towers are 1 and 5/8 inches farther apart at the top than at the bottom, to account for the curve of the earth.

White-Tailed Deer

The graceful white-tailed deer has a reddish-brown coat and a white underside to its tail, which it raises up and flashes as an alarm signal when danger is near. In New York, there are some white-tailed deer that took their name a little too seriously. They are entirely white except for their noses and hooves! That's some good camouflage in the winter.

X-mas

A Christmas tradition in New York, the Tree at Rockefeller Center first took its place in 1931, when construction workers decorated a small tree with strings of cranberries, garlands of paper, and even a few tin cans! Today, the tree can be over a hundred feet tall and covered in 30,000 lights. In 2007, the tree went "green"—after Christmas it was used as lumber for a Habitat for Humanity house.

Yellow Taxi

The first yellow taxis hit the streets of New York City in 1907. Back then there were only 600 taxis, today there are over 13,000. To "hail a cab," all you do is step to the curb and raise your hand when you see a taxi with its light on. Then you jump in, tell them where you are going, and enjoy the ride!

Bronx Zoo

The Bronx Zoo is the largest in-city zoo in the United States with 265 acres of habitats and parklands. It opened on November 8, 1899 with 843 animals and has since expanded to house more than 4,000 animals, many of which are endangered. No wonder almost two million people go to the Bronx Zoo every year to see what all those animals are up to.

Najah Nicholas, age 8

Sanjura Smith, age 12

Cori'Ana Johnson, age 12

Dynasty Ellis, age 7

Thank you to everyone at the Boys & Girls Clubs of Rochester for encouraging your kids to write and enter this contest. Thank you to the dedicated youth development staff who guided the young writers through this process and to Koralee Bernardo for coordinating with the centers. And most of all, thanks to the kids who wrote such fantastic poetry for this book. **Way to go!**

Boys & Girls Clubs of Rochester is a youth development organization aimed at helping young people achieve academic success, develop good character and citizenship, and live healthy lifestyles. Our mission is to inspire and enable young people of all backgrounds to realize their full potential as productive, responsible and caring citizens. The Club provides a safe environment after the school day ends where youth ages 6-18 can engage in a variety of high quality educational and fun programs, activities, and services. To learn more about the Boys & Girls Clubs of Rochester, visit our website at www.bgcrochester.org

Jessmya Kilgore, age 7

Mi'Ron Manley, age 9

Kassidy Plummer, age 8

Diamond Wilson, age 9

Eric Kittles, Jr., age 12

Fajr Good-Knox, age 11

Deanna Higgs, age 8

Text © 2011 by WestWinds Press®

First printing 2011

Library of Congress Control Number: 2011934936

WestWinds Press®
An imprint of Graphic Arts Books
P.O. Box 56118
Portland, OR 97238-6118
(503) 254-5591

Editor: Michelle McCann
Designer: Vicki Knapton

Printed in the United States of America

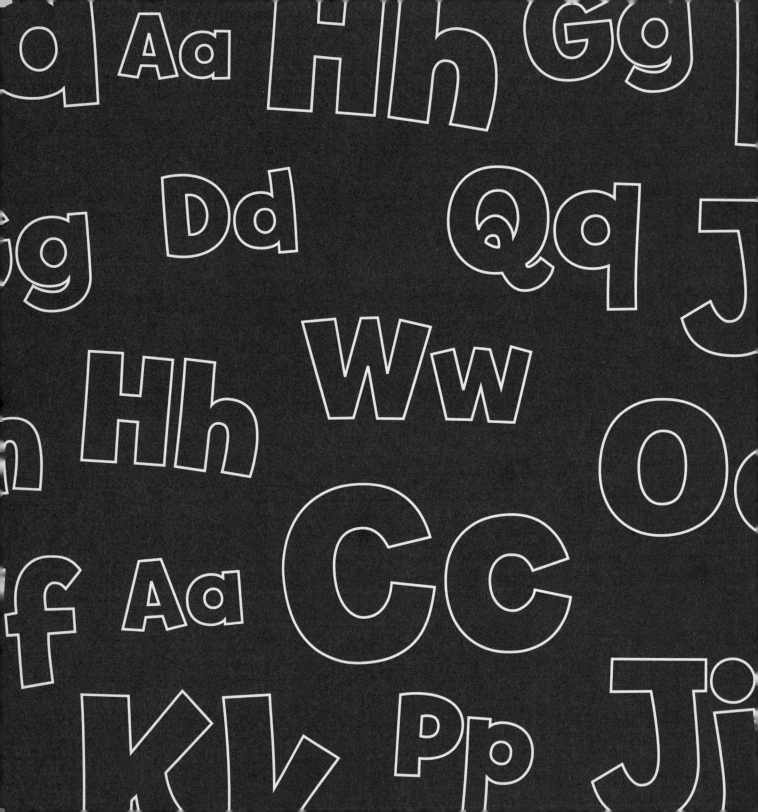